Arabian Nights
TIMELESS SERIES

MAPLE KIDS

TIMELESS SERIES ARABIAN NIGHTS

ALL RIGHTS RESERVED. No part of this book may be reproduced in a retrieval system or transmitted in any form or by any means electronics, mechanical, photocopying, recording and or without permission of the publisher.

Published by

MAPLE PRESS PRIVATE LIMITED
office: A-63, Sector 58, Noida 201301, U.P., India
phone: +91 120 455 3581, 455 3583
email: info@maplepress.co.in
website: www.maplepress.co.in

Reprint 2021 in India

ISBN: 978-93-50337-08-0

Contents

1. Ali The Persian 5
2. The Sultan and the Physician 11
3. Abdul Hassan and the Sultan 18
4. The Cat and the Crow 24
5. The Little Hunchbacked Man 29
6. Monkey Wazir 36
7. Prince of Persia and the Magic Horse 42
8. The Fisherman and the Djinn 49
9. The Blind Beggar of Baghdad 56
10. Sultan Khusaro and the Fisherman 64
11. The Gift 69
12. Sherherazade and Shahriar 74
13. The Sultan and the Falcon 79
14. A Jar of Oil 84
15. Strange Dreams 91
16. The Bull and the Donkey 96
17. The Cock and the Fox 102

Ali the Persian

Sultan Haroun-al-Raschid was restless one night. No matter how hard he tried, he could not sleep. So he sent for his Wazir, Giafar and said, "O Giafar, I feel so sore and heavy hearted. Please arrange for some entertainment so that I may have a sound sleep."

Giafar said, "Your majesty, I have a friend called Ali, the Persian. He is a traveler and has many hilarious stories in his knowledge. If you permit, I will send for him."

The Sultan agreed and Ali, the Persian, was called to the palace.

Ali asked, "My Lord, if you allow, I shall tell you a story that had happened to me once." The Sultan gestured Ali to continue. So he began his story:

Some years ago, I left the city of Baghdad on a journey with a boy who carried a light leather bag for me. We came to a certain city. And as I was buying and selling things there, a wicked Kurd met me and snatching my bag said, "This is my bag and all that is in it is my property."

Arabian Nights

I cried out to the people there, "Please help me. This rascal is out to rob me." For next few minutes, we kept accusing each other for stealing the bag, while a large crowd gathered around us. Finally the folk suggested that we visited the Qazi to settle this quarrel.

We both went to Qazi and explained everything. He asked the Kurd to speak. He said, "This bag is my bag and all that is in it is mine." The Qazi asked him, "When did you lose it?" The Kurd replied, "Only yesterday. I could not sleep the whole night because of it." The Qazi asked, "What is in your bag?"

The Kurd replied, "Two silver styles for eye-powders, and an antimony for the eyes, a kerchief, two gilt cups, two candlesticks, two tents, two platters, two spoons, one cushion, two leather rugs, a brass tray, two basins, a cooking pot, two water jars, a ladle, a needle, a she-cat and two bitches, two sacks, two saddles, a gown, two fur coats, a cow, two calves, a she-goat, two sheep, two lambs, two green pavilions, a camel, two she-camels, a lioness, two lions, a she-bear, two jackals, a mattress, two sofas, an upper chamber, two saloons, a portico, two sitting rooms, a kitchen with two doors and a company of Kurds who will testify that this is my bag."

Then the Qazi asked me, "What do you have to say?" I was surprised at the Kurd's speech. I said, "Lord Qazi, I have only a ruined apartment and another without a door, a dog-house, a boy's school, youths playing dice, tents, tent ropes, city of Basara and Baghdad, the palace of Shaddad bin Ad, an ironsmith's workshop, a fishing net, pickets and one thousand monks who will testify that this is my bag."

When the Kurd heard this, he wept, "This is my bag and it is well known, for in this bag there are castles and citadels, cranes and beasts of prey, men playing chess and draughts, a brood-mare, two colts, a stallion, two blood-steeds, two long lances, a lion, two hares, a city, two villages, a whore, two gallows-birds, a blind man, two witches, a limping cripple, two lamenters, a Christian mercenary, two ministers, a patriarch and a Qazi who will testify that this is my bag."

I was now filled with rage and I said, "I have in this bag a soldier's armour, a broadsword, one-thousand fighting rams, a sheep-fold with its pastures, one-thousand barking dogs, gardens, vines, flowers, sweet smelling herbs, figs, apples, statues, singing women, marriage feasts, tracts of land, a company of daybreak-raiders with swords and spears and bows and arrows, men imprisoned for punishment, a drum, flutes, flags and banners, brides, five Abyssinian women, three

Arabian Nights

Hindu maidens, four girls of Al-Madina, a score of Greek girls, eighty Kurdish girls, seventy Georgian ladies, rivers Tigris and Euphrates, a fowling net, a flint, a multi-colored abacus, one-thousand rogues, horse courses, stables, mosques, baths, builders, a carpenter, a plank, a nail, a black slave, a captain, a caravan leader, cities of Koofaa and Anbar, twenty chests full of stuffs, twenty storehouses, the palace of Kisara Anushirvaan, the Sultandom of Solomon, land from India to Sudan, doublets, clothes and one-thousand sharp razors to shave off the Qazi's beard if he does not accept that this is my bag."

Hearing what we had to say, the Qazi was very confused. He said, "I can see that you two are poisonous fellows, villains, who make fun of Qazis and magistrates and are not afraid of anybody. In the name of Allah, neither from China to Shajarat, nor from Faaras to Sudan or from Waadee Noomaan to Khorasan, was ever heard the things you have told me that this bag contained."

Then the Qazi asked us to open the bag. I opened the bag. It contained only a slice of bread, a lemon, some cheese and olives. I threw the bag down before the Kurd and left.

When the Sultan heard this tale, he laughed till he fell on his back. Ali the Persian was handsomely rewarded for his story.

The Sultan and the Physician

Once upon a time the Sultan of Greece was suffering from a disease called leprosy. Though leprosy can be easily cured today, but in those days it was counted amongst diseases that cannot be cured. The Sultan knew he was about to die but since he was the Sultan he thought, "Why not take a chance and hire the best physicians in the country."

So the Sultan declared that whoever would be able to cure him would be handsomely rewarded for his service. But the ruthless Sultan also announced that if they should fail, they shall be put to death instantly.

First to volunteer were the best physicians of Greece. But they failed and were put to death. Then, the

Arabian Nights

physicians of the neighbouring states volunteered. But they failed too and lost their lives.

Then one fine day a strange old man came to the court and bowed to the Sultan. He said, "I am a physician of a far away land. I have discovered a mix of rare herbs that can cure leprosy. Let me try and I promise I will not disappoint you."

Time was running out for the Sultan. He had no choice but to agree to the physician. He reminded the physician what was waiting for him if he failed. The old physician agreed. On an auspicious day, the physician applied an ointment of rare herbs and wrapped the Sultan in a sheet of cloth. He then asked the Sultan to sleep for few hours. So the sick Sultan slept for the rest of the day and when he got up at dawn he was surprised. The deadly disease that was threatening to kill him was gone. It had vanished like it never happened. The Sultan was impressed.

He invited the physician to a royal feast and after that he handsomely paid the physician and offered him to spend a year at the royal palace. The physician happily agreed as the Sultan had become his good friend.

The Sultan too would often ask the wise physician for advices. But this growing friendship between the Sultan and the old physician made the Wazir jealous. He thought, "If this continues, soon I would lose my

Arabian Nights

job as the Wazir. I have to find a way of sending this old man away from the palace."

So one evening he went to the Sultan and said, "Your majesty, I daresay, I do not trust this physician. There is something about him which tells me that he might be a spy sent by our enemies. I am very sure there is something evil that he is plotting."

The Sultan was furious, "How can you say that without a proof? He is a good old man who has cured me of my disease."

The Wazir said, "He was able to do what so many learned men from our country and the neighbouring states could not. This itself makes me doubt him. Also, we hardly know anything about him. It is my duty as the Wazir to warn you against the danger this man might be putting us all in."

The Sultan was confused. No matter what he said, the Wazir had an argument. Finally the wicked Wazir was able to convince the Sultan that the physician was indeed a spy. So the Sultan ordered the guards to capture the physician and kill him.

When the physician learnt that the Sultan has ordered the guards to kill him, he begged the Sultan to let him go for a day, "Your majesty, I used my precious knowledge of rare herbs to cure you and now you want to kill me as a return to the favour. I think it is very unfair. But then, you are the supreme commander and you know better. However, I pray you give me a day to arrange for the gift that I wish to give you before I die."

The Sultan agreed and the physician set off to arrange for the gift he had promised the Sultan. The next day, he returned with a large book of magic verses and chants. He said, "You majesty, as you cut my head off today, ask your men to place the head on a plate. Then you must turn the pages of this book until you reach the twenty-first page. You must turn each page separately and you must turn them with your own hands. Once you have reached page twenty one, the head will start speaking and it shall then answer anything you ask."

The Sultan heard the physician and then he ordered the chief executioner to cut the man's head off. As the physician's head was cut off and placed on a plate the Sultan began turning the pages of the magic book. He turned one page at a time as he was told, licking his finger to make it moist so that the corner of the pages may stick to it.

The physician had laced the pages of the book with poison. As the Sultan went on licking his finger, the poison kept going into his mouth and from there to his stomach. Soon he felt its effects. As he turned the twenty-first page he began choking. He asked the head, "Why did you do this to me?"

"You are a ruthless and an unfair Sultan. You do not deserve to rule this country," said the head. Then it fell silent. The Sultan died of the poison and no one heard the head talk, ever again.

Abdul Hassan and the Sultan

Once upon a time in the city of Baghdad there lived a very rich businessman. With years, he grew old and one day he died leaving behind everything he owned to his son, Abdul Hassan.

Abdul Hassan was an honest lad. But he fell to keeping company of some evil people who brain washed him into spending all his wealth on them. Abdul Hassan threw lavish parties for his friends and he would drink all day without paying any attention to his father's business. Slowly he lost everything he had. Then one day his friends left him because he was no longer able to throw parties for them like he used to.

It was then Abdul Hassan realized his mistake. With whatever little money he had, he opened a shop for himself and because he was a skilled businessman like his father, he soon

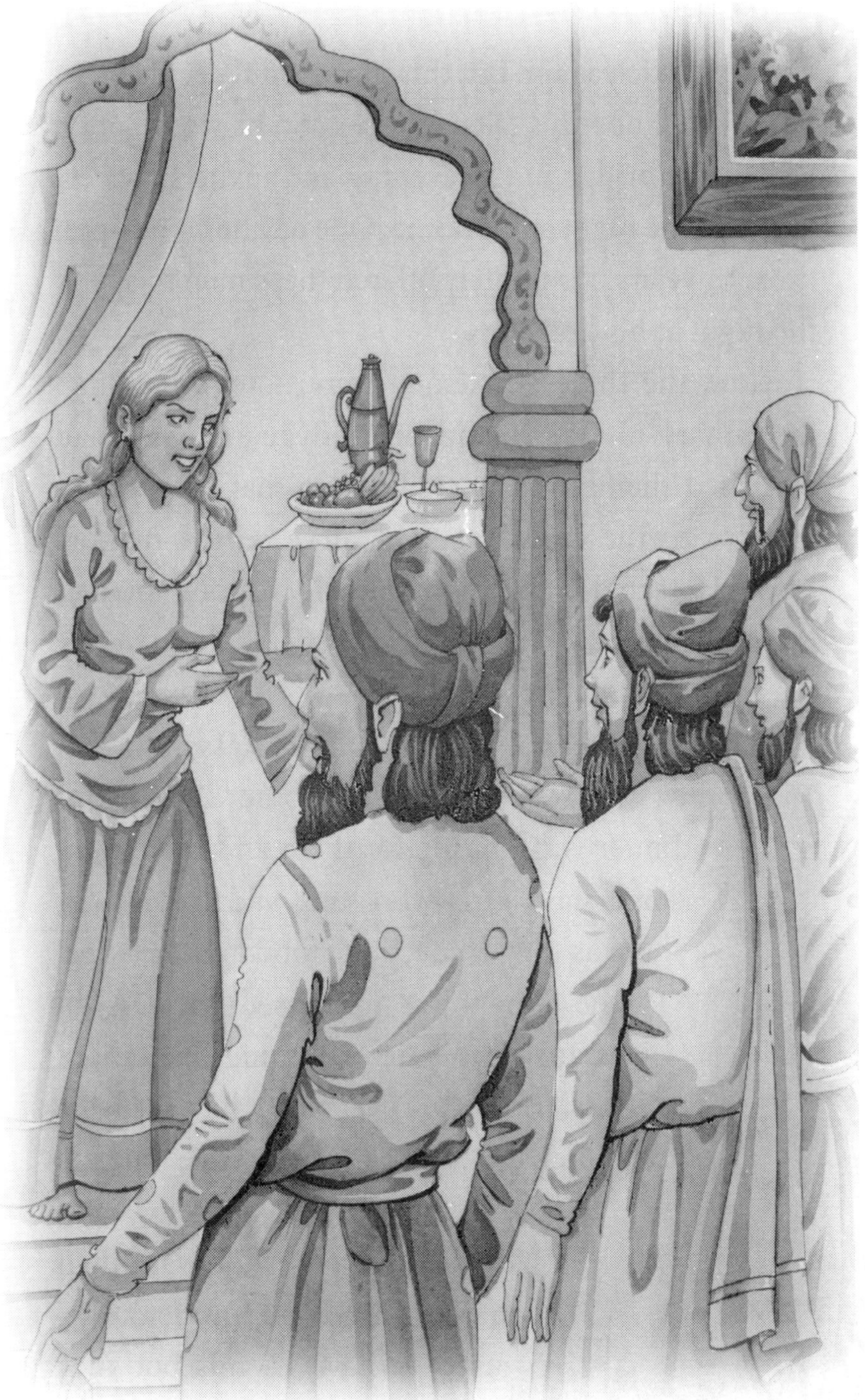

grew to be rich again. But this time Abdul decided that he would choose his friends wisely. So he would often wait at the bridge in the evening and invite strangers to spend the night at his home. One day he came upon three travelers. He politely offered these men to spend the night at his house.

Now, the three gentlemen were none other than the Sultan, his Wazir and his bodyguard. They had disguised themselves as civilians so that they would blend with the crowd as they surveyed the market. Abdul Hassan did not know this. He mistook them as merchants from foreign lands and offered them to stay the night with him.

When the three men reached Abdul Hassan's home, they were welcomed by his mother. A delicious dinner was waiting for them and there were some slave girls who sang and danced for them as they enjoyed the food and the wine.

The Sultan was impressed with Abdul Hassan's hospitality. Learning that Abdul Hassan did this every day, he asked the merchant, "Why do you invite strangers to your home and treat them so well?"

Abdul Hassan who was then drowsy with wine muttered, "I used to have friends but they turned out to be my enemies instead. So I have decided that instead of being nice to evil people like them, I should rather treat strangers. If I was the Sultan for a day I would put all such evil men behind bars."

This amused the Sultan a great deal. He ordered his Wazir to carry Abdul Hassan to the royal palace. He Abdul Hassan was carried to the palace and laid on the Sultan's bed. The Sultan ordered everyone to treat Abdul as the Sultan for a day.

When Abdul woke up he was shocked to find himself in the royal palace. A beautiful slave girl was standing by his bed with his breakfast. And how delicious it smelled!

Abdul was overwhelmed. Did his wish come true? The slave girl said, "People are waiting for your majesty in the court room."

Abdul had his breakfast and changed into the Sultan's robes and turban. He then went down the hall to meet the people in the court room. He spent the rest of the day putting all those guilty behind bars. He even punished some of them with heavy fines. He called in the evil men who were once his friends and sentenced them to fifty lashes.

Arabian Nights

He had a wonderful dinner in the evening and went to bed only to wake up in his humble home the next morning.

Abdul now thought, "Was this a dream? Because I am quite sure it wasn't. I have to find out the truth behind it. He went to the bridge that evening and stood waiting for the three foreign merchants to pass by. After few days they passed by.

The Sultan stopped to greet Abdul, but Abdul just ignored him. The Sultan was offended. "What is the matter, friend?" he asked. Abdul said that it was because of the Sultan that something bad had happened to him. The Sultan was known far and wide for always telling the truth. He confessed that Abdul was right. He had indeed played a prank on the poor man.

Abdul fell at his feet and said, "Your majesty, you must let me stay in your court and serve you." The Sultan agreed.

Abdul Hassan began living in the royal palace from that day. He even got married to the beautiful daughter of a nobleman.

The Cat and the Crow

Once upon a time in a jungle a cat and a crow lived together in peace. They had been best of friends. They were always nice to each other and helped each other during difficulty.

One day as the cat and the crow were sitting under a tree and dining. The crow said, "How wonderful it would be to take a small trip to the mountains." The cat replied, "You can easily fly to the mountains. But it would be years before I walked on these small legs to reach there. Not to mention the dangers that I will meet on my way"

The crow said, "Do not worry my friend, we will think of a way of getting us both to the mountains." They chatted as they had their dinner.

Suddenly, they noticed that a large leopard was coming towards them. Its golden coat gleamed in the sunshine. It was looking straight at them and

Arabian Nights

it stuck out its tongue and smacked its lips. Both the crow and the cat knew, the leopard was coming to eat them up.

Sensing the danger the crow flew to one of the branches. It knew that it could fly away before the leopard could catch it. But the cat was left behind on the ground. The poor cat could not climb a tree because cats are not gifted by God to do that. It began to tremble and as it was almost certain that it was about to die at the hands of the leopard.

The cat called out to the crow, "Dear friend, can't you do something to save me? I do not want to die so early in my life." The cat began to sob. There was no way it could out run the leopard because the leopard was too fast for it. It could not climb the tree and there was no other place to hide.

The crow took pity on his friend. It thought for a while. An idea struck him. He asked the cat not to worry. Near to the tree was a large field of corn. Some farmers and their dogs were working in the field. Determined to save its friend, the crow flew down to one of the dogs and began flapping his wings at the dog's face. This attracted the dog's attention. The playful dog

Arabian Nights

began bounding up and down thinking it would be able to catch the crow. The clever crow began flying towards the tree leading the dog to follow him. The farmers saw the strange sight. Thinking they might lose their dog, they began to chase the dog. Since they were entering the forest, they carried their axes and guns with them.

Very soon they came upon the tree where the cat sat couching with fear. The leopard was quite close to the tree now. The farmers saw it. They with their dogs began chasing the leopard. The poor animal, fearing for its life fled the spot as fast as its legs would carry.

Thus the cat was saved. It thanked the crow for being there when it needed a friend.

The Little Hunchbacked Man

Once upon a time in Baghdad, there lived a tailor. The tailor was a hardworking man. One day there came a little hunchbacked man to his shop, singing and begging for alms. The tailor thought, "What a wonderful voice the little hunchbacked man has. My wife would be so happy to listen to his songs." So the kind tailor invited the little hunchbacked man to his home for dinner.

They reached the tailor's home in the evening, after the tailor has closed his shop. His wife was overjoyed to listen to the little hunchbacked man's songs. They were melodious and very beautiful. The man's voice also was very soft and pleasant to their ears. He played his tabor and they clapped to the tune. They spent the evening, enjoying his songs. "Oh! What a charming fellow!" the tailor's wife exclaimed after he had finished singing. She was indeed very happy to have their guest.

Then it was time for dinner. The tailor's wife had

Arabian Nights

prepared a delicious dish of fish. The little hunchbacked man smacked his lips at the nice aroma of the fish. He had been hungry for many days now. The Tailor and his wife made all efforts to make the little hunchbacked man comfortable.

They were talking over dinner when suddenly the man turned blue. He held his throat with both his hands as if he was choking and then fell unconscious on the floor.

The tailor and his wife were very scared. They bent over his chest and tried to listen to his heart. But there was no sound of thumping. The tailor said, "I think he is dead. He must have choked on a fish bone."

"Oh my God!" the tailor's wife wailed. "What will we do now?"

"Let's leave him at the doctor's house. If anyone found out, they would think the doctor killed him," the tailor said.

So they took the little hunchbacked man to the doctor's house. It was in the middle of the night when they knocked on the doctor's door. The doctor's servant opened the door. The tailor and his wife said, "We have a patient. Please let the doctor know that he should come down immediately."

As the servant went to tell the doctor, the tailor and his wife laid the little hunchbacked man on the stairs and ran away. The doctor put on his robes and he began to hurry down the stairs when he stumbled on the little hunchbacked man lying there.

The doctor checked his pulse. He tried every possible way of reviving him but alas! The little man was dead. The doctor was frightened. "Where did this little man come from? Now he is dead and everyone will think I killed him. I should get rid of this body before the Sultan's guards find out."

So the doctor carried the little man to his neighbour's house. His neighbour was a hard working farmer. The doctor dropped the little hunchbacked man from the chimney and went back to his house.

The little hunchbacked man fell down the chimney with a thud. It woke the farmer. "Who's in there?" he shouted. But there was no answer. He went to check. When he found the little dead man he was shocked, "Where did he come from? He looks like he is dead. If any one finds out, he will think I killed him. I am too young to be hanged to death. I must get rid of him."

So the farmer carried the little hunchbacked man to the streets in the dead of the night and stood him in a dark lane. He then quietly came back home.

An hour later a merchant walked by that road. He had had little too much wine at his friend's house. So he was not in his senses. He saw the little hunchbacked man standing at the corner and thought it was a thief who had come to rob him. He punched the poor dead man and saw the body fall to the ground. The merchant realized that the little hunchbacked man was dead. He began to cry, "Forgive me almighty for I have killed this poor man. I didn't mean to punch him. I wouldn't have punched him if I knew he would die because of it." The merchant sat there with his head in his hands and cried until the Sultan's guards found him in the morning. The guards arrested the poor merchant and produced him before the Sultan.

The merchant confessed that he had killed the little hunchbacked man by punching him. He said he had mistaken the little man to be a thief. The Sultan sentenced him to be hanged because that was the rule of the kingdom.

As the merchant was about to be hanged in public for murder, a loud cry came from the crowd. "Stop, stop! Please don't hang him. He is not guilty but I am. It was I who killed the little hunchbacked man," said the farmer. He came forward and told the Sultan and the crowd the whole story. The Sultan ordered the farmer to be hanged instead of the merchant. So the farmer was dragged to the platform and the rope was put around his neck when another cry

Arabian Nights

came from the crowd. It was the doctor. The doctor came forward and confessed everything. He said that it was he who deserved to be punished and not the farmer.

The Sultan ordered the farmer to be released and instead the doctor was to be hanged. Just then another cry came from the crowd. It was the tailor. The tailor came forward and said, "Your majesty, none of these men are responsible for the little hunchbacked man's murder. I am the one who killed him. I had invited him over to dinner and as we were enjoying the delicious fish my wife had cooked when this man choked on a fishbone and died. Please let all these men go and push me instead."

When the Sultan heard this he laughed. "All right then," he said, "so the little man died of a natural cause. I don't see why any of you is to be blamed. I release all of you."

The doctor came forward and respectfully said, "You majesty, I do not think the little man is dead at all. If you permit me, I will have a look at him." The Sultan nodded and the old doctor went up to the little man. He put his hand in the little hunchbacked man's mouth and drew out the fish bone. The little man gasped for breath and opened his eyes.

"Well done, well done!" the crowd cheered.

Monkey Wazir

Once upon a time, a poet sat under a tree and was trying to compose a poem when suddenly a demon appeared from under the tree. In a thunder like voice it said, "How dare you walk into my land uninvited? This tree is my home. This forest is my property. Since you have come here I have a good mind to curse you!"

The poet begged, "Please good sir, do not harm me. I didn't know that these lands belonged to you. I wouldn't have come otherwise. Please let me go and I promise I will leave immediately."

But the demon was bored. People hardly came near the tree because they all knew that the demon lived there. Thus for many days now, he did not find anyone to play his tricks on. Now that he had an opportunity of causing someone trouble, he was not ready to let go.

So the evil demon, despite the poet's plea turned him into a monkey. Great misfortune fell upon the poor man. When he went home, his mother chased

Arabian Nights

him with a broom shouting, "Damned monkey, go away! Dare you enter my house again! Dare you touch our food!"

Heartbroken, the monkey poet roamed in the streets. People chased him from their homes. Shopkeepers drew out sticks to hit him, if he tried to enter their shops. Little children in the streets threw stones at him. They pointed towards him and laughed.

Life was a curse. Hunger and humiliation made him miserable. The poet decided to live on a tree in an abandoned garden. "Not many people visit this garden anymore so I might be able to live on this tree in peace," he thought.

So the monkey poet began to live on that tree, away from his friends and his mother. He missed them very much.

Now, one day the Sultan declared that he was in need of a Wazir to advice him in the matters of the state. According to the declaration anyone who would be able to write the best letter would be appointed as the royal Wazir. In the next few days, the Sultan received many letters from wise men and scholars across the land. There were so many letters that the Sultan had to spend the next three days reading them. But he was not satisfied. "These are all letters from learned men and masters. But their knowledge is bookish. I need

Arabian Nights

someone who has faced the hardships of life. Only such a person would be able to advice me well," he thought.

Finally one day the Sultan received a letter which truly impressed him. The letter was not very long but it was written in beautiful poetic language and had some very wise advices for the Sultan. He sent for the person who had written that letter to him.

When the person arrived in court everyone was surprised, for he was not a person at all. He was a monkey. The Sultan said to his guards, "What kind of trick is this. I had asked for the person who wrote this letter and you brought along this monkey?"

It was the monkey poet. He now stood in the court with folded hands and said, "Your highness, this is no trick. Indeed, I was the one who had written you that letter. I kept thinking whether or not I should appear in court looking like this. But then you had ordered me to come. How could I refuse you? But I would not advice that you appoint me as your advisor. People will laugh at you if they knew you took advices from a monkey."

The Sultan was humbled by what the monkey poet said. He said, "Do not fear humiliation. I admire your wisdom and your letter was by far the best letter out of all the letters I have received. I shall appoint you as my advisor. But tell me, how did you come to be a monkey?"

The monkey poet then narrated the whole story. The Sultan took pity on him. He called for the royal magician. The magician was very powerful. He at once broke the spell and turned the monkey poet back to his original form. With tears in his eyes, the monkey poet thanked the Sultan for his kindness.

For years the poet served as the Sultan's loyal advisor. The Sultan began to like the handsome poet so much that he offered to marry his daughter to him. Thus the poet became the Sultan's son-in-law and after the Sultan died, he ruled the kingdom with great kindness and justice.

Prince of Persia and the Magic Horse

Once upon a time in Persia, the emperor declared that anyone who would bring him a unique present would have a wish granted. Many rich business men and nobles came to offer the emperor precious stones and statues made of solid gold. But all that failed to impress the emperor.

Then one day a very rich merchant presented him with a statue of a soldier. The emperor asked, "What is so special about this statue?" The merchant said, "Your majesty, this is no ordinary statue. It is magical. Position it at your gates and whenever enemies approach your fort the statue will blow its horn to alert everyone. Come rain, snow or storm, your fort will always remain guarded."

The emperor was impressed. He said, "I admire your present. Tell me what do you wish for in return?" The merchant said, "Your majesty, I wish to marry your eldest daughter." The emperor was more than

Arabian Nights

happy to marry his daughter to the young and wealthy merchant. So they were married and lived happily in the merchant's lavish house.

Soon after, a young scholar visited the emperor. The scholar had brought a silver plate upon which stood a golden peacock and twelve chicks. He explained, "Your majesty, this is not just any plate with golden birds on it. It is a clock. As every hour strikes, the peacock will screech and give a chick a peck. The twelve chicks denote the twelve hours."

The emperor was impressed. "It is a unique clock indeed. What do you wish for in return?" The scholar said, "Your majesty, I wish to marry your second daughter." The emperor agreed and the second daughter was married to the young scholar and they lived happily in the scholar's large mansion.

Then one day an old wizard walked into the emperor's palace. He had brought with him a wooden horse. The emperor said, "You have brought a simple wooden horse as a present. What good is it to me?"

The old wizard said, "Your majesty, this is not just any wooden horse. It has special abilities. It can fly. At your command it will take you anywhere you wish to be within minutes. It might look like an ordinary wooden horse but it is one that truly fits an emperor."

The emperor was impressed again. He asked what the wizard wished for. The wizard said that he wanted to marry the emperor's third and the youngest daughter. The emperor had no choice but to agree. However when the word reached the princess she broke into tears, "Both my sisters got to marry such handsome men. Why does father want me to marry an old man? As much as I wish to obey my father, I can't make myself love the wizard."

Her brother felt sorry for his sister. He told her that he would talk to their father about the marriage. He went to meet the emperor the next day he was amazed to find the old wizard demonstrating the wooden horse to the emperor. The prince said, "Why father? What is so special about this wooden horse that has impressed you so much that you have agreed to marry my sister to this old man?"

The wizard did not like the prince's words. "How dare did he call me old," the wizard thought. He said, "Dear prince, kindly take

Arabian Nights

a ride before you comment about my horse." The prince agreed. He sat on the horse and the wizard said, "If you twist the right ear of the horse, it will begin to fly."

The prince did as he was told and soon he was, swimming through the clouds. It was indeed amazing how swift the horse was. The prince began to enjoy the ride. He steered the horse to dodge the high towers of the city. What an adventure it was!

Down below the emperor was worried. "You didn't tell him how to get down you wicked man. What if he meets with an accident?" No matter how much the emperor's ministers tried to calm him, he just got more and more worried. He ordered the guards to throw the old wizard out of the city.

Meanwhile the prince had reached new lands. He discovered that if he twisted the left ear of the horse, it would bring him back to the ground. The prince landed in what was a royal garden. He began to wonder, "This does not look like Persia. Where am I?"

Then he noticed a palace. He decided to climb the nearest open window. The window led to the room of a beautiful princess. The princess was asleep. She was so pretty that the prince stood by her bed for a long time and gazed at her. He had fallen in love.

Suddenly the princess got up. Seeing a stranger in her room she shrieked. "Guards!" The prince calmly bowed and said, "Do not be afraid, dear princess. I am the prince of Persia. I have lost my way. Please tell me what country is this, so that I can find my way back home."

The princess now noticed how handsome the prince was. She had heard a lot of stories about his bravery. She blushed and said, "This is Greece. But I think you should leave before the guards catch you. My father is a cruel man. He will not spare you if he finds out you had crept into my room while I was asleep."

The guards burst in right then. They tried to capture the prince and a fierce fight broke out. But the brave prince was an exceptional swordsman. The guards were no match for him. Going to the window he whistled for his horse. "Take me with you. Please," the princess cried. The prince lifted her and seated her on the horse. Then he himself mounted the horse and they fled the Royal palace of Greece.

When the prince returned to Persia, his father's joys knew no bounds. He hugged his son and welcomed his new Daughter-in-law. By then the youngest princess had married a nobleman. Together they lived happily ever after.

The Fisherman and the Djinn

Sajid was an old fisherman. He was so poor that he could not afford to provide two meals a day to his children. And he had many children. The children were thin as sticks and they wasted their time playing in the streets as their father could not send them to school.

Poor Sajid was troubled because of this. "How would I ever be able to give my children a good future? I am not a good father," he often thought to himself.

In the name of property he just had an old and ragged fishing boat. Every morning, Sajid would take his boat and go to the sea to catch fish. He would return home in the evening with just one or two fishes, sometimes even empty handed. Life was hard for Sajid and there was no hope that things would improve for him anytime soon.

One day as he was fishing he prayed Allah to grant him a big fish. He cast his net in the water. It was almost

Arabian Nights

noon and the sun was shining with all its might. But he was hard at work.

After some time he pulled his net up. A dead animal was caught in the net. But there was no fish. His heart broke. He threw away the animal and cast his net in the water again. When he lifted back his net this time, he found broken pieces of glass, torn shoes and lots of sea weed in his net but there was no sign of any fish.

Irritated, Sajid cast his net in the water for one last time. He prayed, "Almighty, my children are starving. Won't you care for this one unfortunate man? Please bless me with a fish today. If not for me but at least for the sake of my little, hungry children back home."

And he pulled the net up. More broken glass and weeds were caught in the net but there was no sign of any fish. Sajid noticed a beautiful glass bottle amongst the useless things. The glass bottle looked like it had floated from a very distant land. It was a skillfully crafted small bottle with a golden cap. The cap bore the emblem of Sultan Solomon and was tightly sealed as if to keep what was inside from spilling out.

Sajid thought, "I didn't catch any fish today. But I can still sell this bottle and earn some money. But first I must open the bottle and see what is inside." With his knife he removed the seal from the cap. But as soon as he had unscrewed the cap, the bottle began to quiver.

Arabian Nights

Poor Sajid was so scared that he dropped the bottle and began to tremble. Pink and green smoke issued from the bottle along with a terrible laugh. But Sajid could see no one. "What devil have I released! What is this magic?" he thought to himself.

The smoke now began to take shape and Sajid realized, it was a Djinn. The Djinn was monsterous. It wore thick arm bands made of gold had an evil look in its eye. It said in a booming voice, "Thank you old man, for releasing me from the bottle. I have been trapped in there for almost three hundred years now. For the first hundred years I vowed to make him rich, who would release me. But no one came to my help. Then for the next hundred years I decided I will grant three wishes to the person who released me. But no one came to my help this time too. Finally frustrated, I vowed to kill anyone who released me. And here you are."

Sajid realized he should have sold the bottle without opening it. His curiosity would now lead him to his death. He began to think of a way out.

Clever Sajid said to the Djinn, "You are so big and mighty. I cannot believe you were trapped in this tiny bottle. I wonder even your little finger can fit in the bottle."

The Djinn was offended. It said, "Do not underestimate my powers. I am a Djinn. Anything is possible with my magic." Sajid looked like he doubted it. He said, "No, I can't believe it. You may be whoever, but it is impossible for a huge thing like you to fit inside a tiny bottle as this."

The Djinn was angry now. It said, "So you don't believe me? I will show you how I can fit in that bottle," and it began to turn into smoke again. No sooner the smoke was inside Sajid snatched the cap and set it tightly on the bottle. The Djinn was back in the bottle again. It realized the old man was far too clever for him. It begged Sajid to let it go.

Sajid said, "Are you crazy? I have little children. Who will care for them if you killed me? I should probably throw you back into the sea and tell everyone not to open the bottle if they should find it." The Djinn shed bitter tears. It prayed to Sajid to release it.

Finally the old man took pity on the Djinn. He made the Djinn promise that it will not kill him. Then he unscrewed the cap and let the Djinn go. The Djinn was thankful. It said, "You have helped me so I will offer a reward. Come with me." And it took the fisherman's boat to the hills beyond the seashore. There it led Sajid through a hidden path to a secret cove. It said, "I am going to see the world now. You can fish here as much as you want." And with a gentle shoosh, the Djinn disappeared.

The old fisherman stood staring at the beautiful cove. It was full of colourful fishes. From that day, Sajid's children never went hungry again.

The Blind Beggar of Baghdad

The Sultan of Baghdad Haroun-al-Raschid was strolling in his palace one day thinking about his city and its people when his Wazir, Giafar approached him. Giafar said, "May I remind your highness that today is the day when you had planned to explore the city to make sure that our people are truly happy and content."

Haroun-al-Raschid remembered. He asked his Wazir to get prepared. Both the Sultan and his Wazir dressed as foreign merchants set off for the markets of the city. They had just crossed the narrow channel and stepped off from their boat when a blind old beggar caught the Sultan's wrist. "Please give this poor man some alms. Allah will answer your prayers." The Sultan was a kind man. He drew some money out of his pockets and handed them to the beggar. But the beggar refused to let go. He said, "If the good man must give me money, he must also punch me in the face."

The Sultan and his Wazir were amazed. What kind of man requests a stranger to beat him? The Sultan said, "Old man, Take more money if you must but do not ask me to be so cruel. You have not harmed me. Therefore if I hit you, it will be so unfair."

But the old beggar continued to beg the Sultan to hit him. Finally, the Sultan agreed. He said, "All right I will punch you in the face. But you have to promise that you will visit the Sultan in his palace tomorrow." The beggar was desperate to get beaten. He agreed what the Sultan said, got punched in the face and went away with the money.

The Sultan said to his Wazir, "What kind of trade was that? I feel so miserable having to hit that poor man." Giafar said, "Your highness, I believe there is a reason behind his odd behavior. We shall find out tomorrow if he remembers to pay us a visit."

The Next day, after the evening prayers, the beggar appeared in the Sultan's palace. The Sultan asked, "What is your name old man? And what is the story behind your strange behavior?"

The beggar bowed and said, "Your highness, my name is

Arabian Nights

Baba Abdallah. I was born to rich parents in Baghdad. But when I was very young, both my parents died. They had left behind some money for me. Yet life was difficult as an orphan. Slowly I learnt how the world works and when I came of age, I bought eighty camels with that money. I began to let people hire my camels and that was how I earned my living. But one day, something happened which completely changed my life."

The Sultan and his Wazir were listening very intently to Baba Abdallah's story. Tears were flowing from the old man's blind eyes as he remembered that day. Baba Abdallah continued his story:

One day as I was travelling home from Balsora, I met a Fakir on my way. I offered the poor man some food because he seemed very hungry. After he had eaten he said, "Bless you my child. You have treated me nicely. I will share a secret with you. I know the location of a treasure. There is so much silver and gold and precious stones there that you will fall short of camels."

I was excited. The Fakir continued, "Come with me and I will show you. But first you will have to promise that you will give me half of your camels. You give me forty camels and I will make sure that you be so rich as to buy thousand more."

Arabian Nights

I had no choice but to agree. We walked for miles until we came to some hills. We could see a passageway through the hills. We began to walk through the passageway. It led us to a cave. We went inside the cave and there it was! Vast heaps of gold coins and precious stones lay around us. I was overwhelmed with joy. I began to fill my bags with the treasure and load them onto my camels.

But the Fakir was not interested in picking up the treasure. He walked around the cave and came upon an old dusty vase. He put his hand in the vase and drew out a small casket which he then hid under his robes. I asked, "What is in the casket which is so precious that you do not care about the amazing treasure?"

"Oh it is nothing. Just some ointment to soothe my old joints," he said. I knew he was lying. I loaded the camels and we set for Baghdad.

After we had walked some distance, the Fakir said, "This is where I have to take your leave. Give me the camels you had promised and we shall never see each other again."

Even though I was very rich now but the thought of losing my forty camels made me sad. I began to chalk a plan in my mind. I said, "Old man, what will you do with forty camels. You do not have the experience of handling a camel."

The Fakir considered this. He said, "You are right. Just give me ten camels then." I continued my argument and explained to him how difficult it will be to handle even ten camels. He finally gave up. "I will not have any camel then. But I must bid you farewell now. Have a good life."

But I was not satisfied yet. I wanted to know what was in the small casket that he had hidden under his robes. He said it was a magical ointment. "What use is magic to you? You have only few years of your life left. Give me the casket." I was beginning to get rude but the Fakir was calm. He said, "Fine then, you can have the ointment too. But let me explain how it works. If you put some on your left eye you will be able to see all the hidden treasures of the world." This excited me so much that I snatched the casket from him and smeared the ointment on both my eyes.

And that was the last I saw of the world. Everything began to fade away and slowly darkness was the only thing I could see. I was blind. The Fakir said, "You took away the camels you promised, I did not say anything. You took away the casket of ointment I did not say anything. But you are so greedy that you didn't even wait for me to finish. The ointment only works if you apply it to your left eye. But if by accident you apply it to your right eye instead, you will be blinded for life."

The Fakir rode away with my camels and my treasure as I stood in the middle of the desert, blinded by the magical ointment. I deserve to be beaten. I have been such a selfish man.

The Sultan and his Wazir felt pity for the blind beggar. The kind Sultan said, you have realized your mistake, Baba Abdallah. Now you should forgive yourself and try to live in peace. From that day the Sultan sent a little money for Baba Abdallah's upkeep while the old man having forgiven himself lived to tell everyone, how bad it was to be so greedy.

Arabian Nights

Sultan Khusaro and the Fisherman

Once a fisherman approached Sultan Khusaro's court and presented to him a very beautiful fish. The fish was twice the size of an ordinary fish and it gleamed in the light from the beautiful chandelier above as if it was studded with precious stones. The Sultan was impressed as he had never seen a fish as grand as this. He offered four thousand Dirhams to the fisherman. The fisherman bowed with gratitude.

However, the queen was upset. She said, "What is the point of giving such a huge amount of money to this poor fisherman for a single fish? I am afraid you are setting a bad example for the people. Everyone would think you spend money like it had no value. Then everyone in your court would expect that you gave such expensive gifts to them."

Arabian Nights

The Sultan agreed with his queen. He had indeed paid the fisherman more than what he deserved. But he had already given the fisherman the money. How could he ask it back? The Queen suggested that he asked the fisherman whether the fish is male or a female. If the fisherman said it was male, he should say he wanted a female fish and if the fisherman said it was a female, he should say he wanted a male fish. Thereby return the fish and get the money back.

So the Sultan asked the fisherman if it was a male or a female fish. Though the fisherman did not hear what the queen had to say, he was very wise. He said, "Your majesty, the fish is neither male nor female. It is a hermaphrodite."

The Sultan was much impressed by the fisherman's wit. He offered the man another four thousand Dirhams. The queen grimaced.

As the fisherman received the money from the treasurer, one of the coins fell to the ground. The fisherman then stooped down and picked it up. The queen said to the Sultan, "Do you see how greedy he is. You have given him eight thousand Dirhams but he couldn't leave behind that single coin that dropped to the floor. If he had left it there some poor servant of the court could have made use of it."

Arabian Nights

The Sultan could see a point in the queen's words. He asked the fisherman, "Dear fellow, why did you pick up that coin which had fallen on the floor. Had you left it there some poor man could have made use of it."

The fisherman said, "Your majesty, I did not pick up the coin because I am a greedy man. I picked it up because it had your picture on one side and your name on the other. How could I leave the coin on the floor knowing that some ignorant man might step on it bringing dishonour to you?"

The Sultan burst out laughing this time. He admired the fisherman's wit and wisdom. He knew, the fisherman truly deserved to be paid handsomely not just for his fish but for his cleverness.

The Gift

Once upon a time in Baghdad lived a man called Hamid. Though Hamid was a hardworking man, he had lost all his wealth and was neck deep in debts. Hamid was in desperate need of money as the lenders were threatening to kill him if he didn't return the money he owed them. It was becoming difficult to live in Baghdad with each passing day.

One day Hamid decided to leave his home and travel to other cities. "You never know. My fortunes may change in a new city." So he set off. As Hamid had no money he could not afford to buy a horse or a carriage. So he walked for days. Finally he reached a city which had very high walls around it.

Hamid was very tired and hungry. He had not eaten for a very long time. He walked to the nearest house and fell on its stairs. As Hamid was resting, he suddenly smelled food. The house had belonged to a very

Arabian Nights

rich man. His servant was carrying food for his dog. Hamid noticed the plate made of gold in the servant's hand which now smoked with hot food. He also noticed the dog which was tied to one of the pillars near to where he was sitting. The dog wore a thick golden collar.

Hamid's mouth began to water to see the tasty meat that was laid before the dog. Suddenly the dog withdrew. With its snout it pushed the plate towards Hamid. Clearly, it wanted Hamid to eat its food.

Hamid was overjoyed. He quickly ate the food, leaving some for the dog. But the dog refused to eat even that. It kept pushing the plate towards Hamid as if to say "Take the plate with you."

Hamid took the plate and left the city. When he reached another city, he sold the gold plate and got a handsome price for it. He then started a business and soon he had enough to pay his debts with. Hamid became a successful businessman.

But he never forgot the dog. One day he decided to visit the city. He bought a present for the dog and the dog's owner and rode to the city with the high walls. When he reached there, he found that the large house now stood in ruins. An old man sat on the stairs now. He looked pale and wretched.

"Good day sir, Can you tell me where may I find the person who owned this house?" Hamid asked the

Arabian Nights

old man. "Alas! I am the wretched fellow who owned this place," the old man said. He continued when he noticed the expressions of shock on Hamid's face. "Yes, about an year ago there was a terrible fire. I lost everything in that fire. I am ruined now. This place used to be so magnificent!"

Hamid felt sorry for the man. He said, "I was here few years ago. Your dog had sacrificed his food for me. It was because of your generous dog that I have been able to pay my debts and be successful in my business today. I have brought a present for you. And here is some money. Please accept it."

The old man shook his head, "I cannot accept the price of a gift that my dog had made to you." And with this he got up and left. Tears came to Hamid's eyes. He vowed to always remember the old man's act of kindness and selflessness.

Sherherazade and Shahriar

Many years ago a large kingdom stretched from Persia to China. It went through India and reached the borders of China and was ruled by a royal and mighty dynasty for four hundred years. During the days when this kingdom flourished with prosperity, a very kind-hearted Sultan ruled over it with justice.

This Sultan had two sons. They were called Shahriar and Shahzaman. The brothers had great love and respect for each other. When their father died, the elder brother Shahriar took up the throne. He declared his younger brother as the ruler of Samarkhand, a great territory of the Persian Empire.

The brothers ruled wisely like their father and peace prevailed in their kingdoms for many years. Sultan Shahriar took a beautiful woman as his Sultana. He loved the Sultana more than his life. He would often deck her with the most precious jewels in the empire and the Sultana had everything

Arabian Nights

that she desired, brought to her by the royal servants.

They lived in prosperity and happiness for some years until the Sultan found that his wife had been unfaithful. Mad with rage he drew his sword and killed his wife at once. And for many years after that he mourned her death and disloyalty.

The heartbroken Sultan, Shahriar, decided to avenge himself. Since he thought all women were disloyal, he decided to marry a maiden each day and then kill her the next morning. The Sultan who was once kind and loved turned into someone his people began to fear. They were angry for their beautiful daughters were no longer safe in the kingdom.

One day the Wazir's elder daughter Sherherazade said to her father, "Father, the Sultan's cruel practice has to be stopped. If I am able to mend his broken heart lot of lives can be saved. But for that I would have to marry him."

The Wazir was shocked to hear this. "Dear daughter, I have raised you up with so much love and care. I can't willingly send you to your doom. A father's heart breaks to even think of it."

But brave Sherherazade was convinced that she could stop the bloodshed. So the Wazir had to give in to her desires and he got her married to the Sultan. The next day, the

Arabian Nights

Sultan married Sheherazade in grand fan fare. As a gift in marriage, Sheherazade asked her father if her sister Dinarzade could accompany her to the palace. Sheherazade asked her sister to beg her to tell a story every night.

So Dinarzade like an obedient sister came to the Sultan and his bride that night and said, "Dear sister, one last time will you tell me one of those fascinating stories you know?"

The Sultan exclaimed in surprise, "A story?"

Sheherazade asked the Sultan if he wanted to hear a story. The Sultan was fascinated and he agreed. So the beautiful Sheherazade began to tell a story.

The clever Sultana would stop the story at the crack of dawn when she would ask both the Sultan and her sister to go to bed. The Sultan excited to find out the rest of the story would spare her life for the day. This went on for the next thousand and one nights.

The Sultan's heart was slowly mended and he grew to be in love with Sheherazade. He stopped killing young maidens of the city and remained married to Sheherazade until the very last day.

The thousand and one stories that Sheherazade told her husband, the Sultan and her sister, Dinarzade later spread far and wide through wise travelers and came to be known as the Arabian Nights.

The Sultan and the Falcon

Once upon a time, there lived a Sultan. He was very brave and kind. He favoured justice and everyone loved him for his generosity.

The Sultan had a pet falcon. The bird was like a constant companion to the Sultan. Wherever the Sultan went the bird would go with its master. One day the Sultan went into the forest with some of his men to hunt. The falcon too went with them. It was a hot summer day but the forest was so dense that hardly any sun rays entered it.

The falcon began to circle the forest. Suddenly it spotted a deer. "Follow the deer!" the Sultan encouraged his men. He was a passionate hunter and chasing a deer was one of the sports he enjoyed.

The Sultan turned around his beautiful white horse and

Arabian Nights

Arabian Nights

galloped behind the deer. The deer too was young and quick. It began to make its way through the thick bushes. The Sultan skillfully rode through the bushes to catch up. The falcon was circling above them in the mean time.

Suddenly the deer took a big leap across a little pond and got away. The Sultan and his horse could not cross the pond. Irritated the Sultan got down from his horse. When he looked around there was no one to be found. In his pursuit of the deer his men had been left far behind.

The Sultan now stood beside the pond, alone and lost. He thought, "Now that I am standing near this pond I might as well have a drink of water before I set off to look for a way back." He bent down, folded his sleeves and as soon as he had taken some water from the pond in his cupped hands the falcon flew down to him and began flapping its wings at the Sultan's face. The Sultan was so surprised that he let the water slip through his fingers.

The Sultan was kind. He did not say anything to the falcon. He cupped his hands again and took some water from the pond. But the bird just wouldn't let him do that. It flapped its wings and began pecking at the Sultan's fingers.

Arabian Nights

The Sultan was upset. "Damned bird, what is the matter with you?" he said to the falcon.

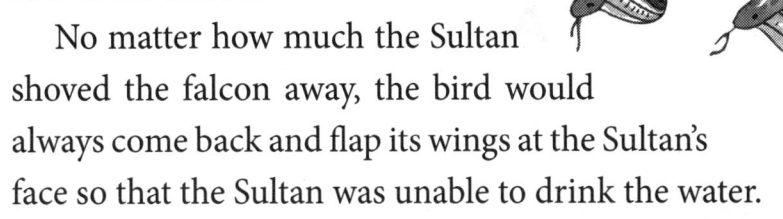

No matter how much the Sultan shoved the falcon away, the bird would always come back and flap its wings at the Sultan's face so that the Sultan was unable to drink the water.

At one point the falcon gave a sharp nip on the Sultan's hand. This was enough to get the Sultan to draw his sword. "Enough is enough! You do that again and I will slice you into tiny pieces of meat," he threatened the bird.

The falcon calmed down. It perched on the Sultan's arm and looked towards the sky. The Sultan was confused. But when he followed the falcon's gaze, it became all clear. Right behind him was a sandalwood tree. The branches of the tree hung above him like a roof. Thousands of snakes hung from the branches. Their mouths were wide open and poison dropped from them into the pond.

Had the Sultan put the water from the pond to his lips, he would have died instantly from the poison. The falcon had saved his life. The Sultan was thankful to the bird. He let the falcon lead the way and returned to his palace just when the sun was about to set.

A Jar of Oil

Many years ago, during the reign of Sultan Haroun-al-Raschid a business man named Ali Khwaja lived in Arabia. Though Ali Khwaja was not very rich, he earned enough to be able to get by comfortably.

Ali Khwaja lived with his old parents. He never got married. So when his parents died he was left alone. Loneliness began to haunt him so much that he began to have nightmares. Ali Khwaja decided to go on a holy pilgrimage. "Only if I surrender myself to God will I find peace," he thought.

He packed his things and planned to leave. But just then he remembered about his savings. Though Ali Khwaja was not very rich, he was a hardworking man. He had saved ten thousand gold coins for future use. He thought, "I think five thousand gold coins will be enough for the trip. I have to carefully store the remaining five thousand gold coins so that no one steals it."

Arabian Nights

Ali Khwaja bought an earthen jar and placed the coins in it. He then filled the jar with oil and sealed it. He decided to leave the jar with his best friend Abdul Hassan. He went to Abdul's house and knocked on the door. "Good evening dear friend," Abdul received his friend with a warm smile. "But what brings you here?" he asked Ali Khwaja.

"I have decided to go on a pilgrimage. So I thought I should say good bye to you before I leave." "That is great news. Prayers will benefit you. After all Allah is our only company in old age. Is there anything I can do for you? Anything you need?" Abdul said.

Ali Khwaja replied, "I have everything I need. But there is one favour I must ask from you. Will you keep this jar of oil with you until I return?" Abdul Hassan was worried that Ali Khwaja might end up asking for money. Abdul Hassan was a big miser.

But he heaved a sigh of relief when he learnt that his friend didn't need to borrow anything from him. "Of course, you may leave it in my store room until you return," he said. So Ali Khwaja left the jar of oil in Abdul Hassan's store room and set off for the pilgrimage. He told Abdul that he would return in five months and take the jar away.

Three months passed. One evening, Abdul Hassan's servant came to him saying they had run out of oil and there was no way they could light the lamps. Abdul said, "Open Ali Khwaja's jar. I will take some oil out of it now and replace it tomorrow. He will never find out." So Abdul Hassan's servant opened the jar when Abdul Hassan exclaimed in surprise, "What is this? Gold coins? Bless my soul, that fool has stored gold coins in a jar of oil!"

Abdul was so tempted that he poured out the oil from the jar and took the gold coins from it. He then replaced the oil in the jar and sealed it like before.

Ali Khwaja returned after five months, just as he had promised. He went to Abdul Hassan's house and to fetch his jar of oil. But when he reached home and opened the jar he was shocked. The five thousand gold coins were gone. Ali ran to the Sultan and fell at his feet with tears in his eyes. "Your majesty, I have been robbed. I had worked day and night to save five thousand gold coins which I then left with my friend when I went to the pilgrimage. But they have vanished now. That money was to support me in my old age. What will I do now that it is gone?" he sobbed.

Arabian Nights

The Sultan heard the whole story. He then sent for Abdul Hassan. "This poor man's money vanished only after he had left it with you. If you have taken it, return it immediately."

Abdul Hassan was cunning. He said, "Your Majesty, with God's grace my business is successful. Why will I steal someone else's money? Ali Khwaja had left the jar sealed and when he got it back, it was still sealed in the same way. Was it not?" Ali Khwaja nodded. Abdul continued, "Then how can you blame me for the theft? I wasn't even aware that he had left five thousand gold coins in that jar. He didn't tell me that when he left the jar with me. The jar might as well have been empty. He is lying, your majesty, so I am forced to give him five thousand gold coins."

The Sultan was confused. He could not decide who was guilty. He decided to dismiss the case for the time being. The news spread and everyone began to discuss Ali and Abdul's case. One day when the Sultan was riding through the market, he noticed some children enacting the case as a game. Two of them played Ali and Abdul. One of them played the Sultan himself. The Sultan stood and watched the kids. Suddenly he had an idea.

He returned to the palace and sent for both Ali Khwaja and Abdul Hassan. He then ordered for the richest oil merchant in the city. When the oil merchant arrived, the Sultan asked, "How well do you recognize oil?" The oil merchant said, "Your majesty, I have been in the oil business for forty years now. I can tell everything about oil just by smelling it. I developed the skill so that I don't get cheated in my business."

Then the Sultan asked again, "Can tell how old a certain sample of oil might be?" The oil merchant said he could. So Ali Khwaja's jar of oil was brought in. The merchant sniffed the oil in the jar and said, "Your majesty, this oil is no more than two months old."

"This is not possible. Ali Khwaja was away for five months. This proves someone must have replaced the oil while he was gone." The Sultan said. Abdul Hassan remained silent. He was punished for his crime while Ali Khwaja got back the money he had lost.

Arabian Nights

Strange Dreams

Once upon a time in Bagdad, there lived a very hard working man called Shayeed. But misfortune fell on him one day and he was told that several of his ships never made it to the land. The man had taken huge loans to buy those ships and as they sank in the sea, he lost all his wealth repaying those loans.

He became very poor and could not afford the luxuries like before. His wife left him and went back to her father's house. Hungry and heartbroken, he sat in his verandah one day and began to think, "My life is ruined. I wish I had not borrowed so much money to invest in the ships. If only I could get back the money I have lost, I promise to be wise this time."

Sleep came over him. He closed his eyes and soon began to dream. In his dream a voice told him to go to Cairo. It said, his life was about to change. When he got up could not believe his dream. He thought,

Arabian Nights

"I should take a chance and go to Cairo. I have lost whatever there was to lose. My money is gone. My wife has left me. If nothing, I will at least get to see a new city."

He set off for Cairo. When he reached the city he was puzzled. The people there dressed differently, they spoke different language. Shayeed walked around the city all day. Finally as he was tired, he lay down on the stairs of a mosque and slept.

That night, few thieves came into the mosque. The owner and his guards chased the thieves but the thieves were quick and they got away. When the owner and his guards saw Shayeed sleeping on the stairs they caught him and threatened to kill him for being a thief.

Shayeed began to tremble. He said, "Please let me go. I am a poor man from Baghdad. I travelled to Cairo because a dream told me to. I am innocent." The owner began to laugh, "What nonsense! You believe in dreams, do you? What a fool you are. I had a dream last night that a house in Baghdad which has a marble fountain in its garden had a treasure hidden under the fountain. Do you think I believe that? It was just a dream. Go back to Baghdad. There is nothing in Cairo for you."

The owner and his guards released Shayeed. After what

Arabian Nights

happened, he was too scared to stay in Cairo. He travelled back to Baghdad.

When he came back to Baghdad, Shayeed realized that the only house in Baghdad which had a marble fountain in its garden was his house. He decided to dig under the fountain and see. That evening he took a hammer and removed the fountain. Then he dug the spot. After hours of digging, he suddenly hit on something. When he pulled it out he saw it was a chest full of gold coins and precious jewels.

Shayeed was overjoyed. He invested some of it in a good business and soon grew to be rich. He realized why his dream had told him to go to Cairo.

The Bull and the Donkey

Once upon a time in Baghdad, there lived a merchant. He was a very honest man. Because he was so kind towards the poor people of the city, Allah had blessed him with a strange ability. He could understand the language of the animals. But the merchant chose not to disclose this to anyone. So nobody knew about this talent of his. Not even his wife.

The merchant had a bull and a donkey. Because he owned some acres of land, the merchant often hired peasants to grow some crops on those lands and to sell them in the market. The bull was used to plough the lands.

One day the merchant heard the bull say to the donkey, "All under you is clean and fresh, men wait upon you, they feed you sifted barley, they give you clean water to drink; while I am led in the middle of the night, they set the plough on my neck, and I get tired working in the fields from morning till evening.

Arabian Nights

After that they ill-treat me, shut me up in a shed and throw me beans and crushed straw mixed with dirt and I lie in dirt. I am always kept hungry while you are given food to your fill."

The donkey said, "You are ill treated because you are a fool. Here let me give you an advice. The next time they come to set the plough on your neck, shake your head and do not let them put that around you. When they drag you away, just refuse to go with them. When they throw beans before you, do not touch it. Your condition will improve, my friend."

As the bull's life was already miserable, it decided to try the donkey's advice. So the next day when the peasants came to put the plough around the bull's neck he shook his head and threw them off. When they tried to drag him to the fields it bent its legs and sat down, refusing to go. The peasants thought, "May be the bull is not feeling well. We must inform the master." So they went to the merchant and told him everything. The merchant however, knew everything already. He said, "If the bull is not feeling well, let us give him a day to rest. Instead, put the plough on

Arabian Nights

the donkey and make him do the bull's work today."

So the peasants put the plough on the donkey and took him to the fields. The poor donkey had to work in the fields all day. When it came back into the shed the bull was waiting to receive his friend. "You are indeed very wise dear friend. I have rested all day and have been fed well. They have even cleaned my shed. I feel so good. I plan to repeat this tomorrow too."

All hell broke loose for the donkey. "That would mean another day of back-breaking work. My legs are hurting and my eyelids are sore already. I can't stand this!" he thought.

He said to the bull, "Dear friend, you do believe what I say is for your own good, don't you?" The bull nodded. "Then listen," the donkey continued, "I overheard the master saying to one of the peasants that if your condition doesn't improve and you continue to be sick, he'd have no choice but to sell you to the butcher. That means you will be sent to the slaughter house to be killed. I would recommend you play nice and resume your work at the fields tomorrow."

The bull was shocked. In no way was he prepared to be sold to the butcher and sent to the slaughter house. When the next morning dawned, the peasants were surprised to see the bull already to be taken to work.

The merchant laughed to himself. He knew what must have happened in the night.

The Cock and the Fox

One bright evening as the sun was sinking on a glorious world a wise old Cock flew into a tree to roost. Before he composed himself to rest, he flapped his wings three times and crowed loudly. But just as he was about to put his head under his wing, his beady eyes caught a flash of red and a glimpse of a long pointed nose, and there just below him stood Master Fox.

"Have you heard the wonderful news?" cried the Fox in a very joyful and excited manner.

"What news?" asked the Cock very calmly. But he had a queer, fluttery feeling inside him, for, you know, he was very much afraid of the Fox.

"Your family and mine and all other animals have agreed to forget their differences and live in peace and friendship from now on forever. Just think of it! I simply cannot wait to embrace you! Do come down,

Arabian Nights

dear friend, and let us celebrate the joyful event."

"How grand!" said the Cock. "I certainly am delighted at the news." But he spoke in an absent way, and stretching up on tiptoes, seemed to be looking at something afar off.

"What is it you see?" asked the Fox a little anxiously.

"Why, it looks to me like a couple of Dogs coming this way. They must have heard the good news and—"

But the Fox did not wait to hear more. Off he started on a run.

"Wait," cried the Cock. "Why do you run? The Dogs are friends of yours now!"

"Yes," answered the Fox. "But they might not have heard the news. Besides, I have a very important errand that I had almost forgotten about."

The Cock smiled as he buried his head in his feathers and went to sleep, for he had succeeded in outwitting a very crafty enemy.